ALBERT'S CHRISTMAS

ALBERT'S CHRISTMAS

by

ALISON JEZARD

Illustrated by

MARGARET GORDON

LONDON

VICTOR GOLLANCZ LTD

1970

First published October 1970
Second impression November 1970

ISBN 0 575 00511 4

Printed in Great Britain by
The Camelot Press Ltd., London and Southampton

For my friends Susette and Diana

CONTENTS

I

ALBERT THE POSTMAN

Albert stretched his toes to the cheerful fire and gazed out of the window of his cosy little basement bed-sitting room. He could see the legs of the people hurrying past and it seemed to him that they were all very busy *doing* something.

Albert looked round at his room. It was all sparkling clean, the brass knobs on the bed and the fender shining bright, and his Grandfather's marble clock dusted. The patchwork cover on his bed was freshly washed and all the furniture had been polished. There wasn't anything to do at home and there weren't many places he could go to on a cold December day.

"I think I would like to have a job of some sort," said Albert to himself. "Just for a little while, to see what it's like. I might earn some extra money for Christmas presents." He thought about it. "What could I do at Christmas time. *I* know! Postmen! They always have more postmen at this time of year. I'll go round there straight away." And Albert put on his scarf, pulled his cap down firmly on to his ears, clumped up the eight steps from his basement room at 14 Spoonbasher's Row, and set off down the road to the post office.

He went round to the back of the building and spoke to a man in a navy-blue uniform.

"Excuse me." He raised his cap politely. "Do you need any extra postmen this Christmas?"

The man looked at Albert and thought for a moment, then he asked, "Do you think you could carry a heavy bag?"

"Oh, yes, I'm quite strong, really I am."

"Do you know the streets round here?"

"Yes, I know them all very well indeed. I've always lived here."

"Well," said the man, "we *do* need help. In fact we need it right away. How soon could you start?"

"Right away!" Albert told him cheerfully.

"Come on, then," and the man led Albert into the big room where all the letters and parcels were sorted ready for delivery. There were a great many people very busy indeed putting parcels into different mail-bags, and letters into the right boxes for each road.

"We must make you a postman first," said the man and he fastened round Albert's arm a blue band which had on it a red circle with the words "Post Office Postman" and the number 56. "Wait here a minute," he said.

Albert stood and waited watching all the bustle around him and feeling quite important. He looked down at the armband. "Post Office Postman," he said to himself. "I must show this to Henry."

The man came back carrying a bag and a sheet of paper. "Look," he said, "this is the route for you to take this morning." He began to draw a sketch. "You go down Butler's Walk, into Cutler Lane and finish up with Spoonbasher's Row."

"That's where *I* live," said Albert, excitedly.

"Oh, well, you'll be all right then," and he added, "I'll just make a note of your name and address and then you can get along."

And so, feeling very proud of himself, Albert marched out of the post office with his bag over his shoulder.

He took out the first bundle of letters, which were already sorted into the right order for him, and read, "Mrs Cornwall, 2 Butler's Walk". He looked for number 2 and pushed the letter in through the letter-box. Next there were three letters for number 4 and an interesting looking little parcel for number 8. Albert shook the parcel and prodded it and then he looked all round him in case anyone had seen him and hurriedly rang the bell. A nice lady came to the door and Albert said, "Parcel for you," and the lady said, "Thank you very much." Then she looked at him and added, "You're Albert, aren't you? I've often seen you in Petticoat Lane doing your shopping. Are you a postman now?"

"Only for Christmas," Albert told her.

"Oh, well, I'll be seeing a bit more of you. I mustn't keep you."

Albert trotted on up and down steps and in and out of gates until the bag began to feel a lot lighter and then he took out a letter with a funny-looking stamp on it. "Albert, 14 Spoonbasher's Row," he read. "That's me!" He looked more closely at the stamp and it had the word "Australia" on it.

Then Albert remembered the Koala bear he had met when he was in Kent with Henry. Henry was the horse who pulled Mr Higgins' rag and bone cart and he had pulled a gypsy caravan for Albert. In Canterbury they had met Digger the Koala, and later on Digger had come to visit Albert in London.

"I won't look at it now," Albert told himself as he climbed down the eight steps to his basement room and pushed the letter through his own box. When he reached the street again he looked at the next letter and found that *it* was for him too! This time it had the postmark "Stirling" and he knew it was from his cousin Angus. Back he went down the steps with the second letter and then he hurried along the street to finish the rest of his deliveries.

When it was all done he took the empty bag back to the post office and arranged to start early the next morning. Then, tired but feeling very happy, he collected his own shopping bag from where he had left it in a corner and set off for the shops to buy something for his tea.

When he had bought his bread and butter and cheese and a tin of sardines, he went into the greengrocer's for some oranges and there he saw a beautiful little Christmas tree, already set in a small blue pot.

"I'll buy that and put it on the table," Albert told himself. "It would look lovely there and I can afford to buy a few extra things now that I'm working."

Albert paid for the tree and went to find a shop where he could buy decorations for it. He chose some pretty, coloured glass balls and some silver tinsel and a bright shining gold star to put on the top.

Albert could hardly carry everything but he just managed to stagger home with his load. He opened the door and there, on the floor, were the two letters.

"Oh, look, the postman's been," he chuckled.

When he had put all his shopping down on the table and filled the kettle for a cup of tea, he opened his letters. The first one, from Digger in Australia, was a Christmas

card which had on it a picture of a kangaroo wearing a paper hat and standing beside a Christmas tree. Inside were the words, "Happy Christmas, Cobber, with love from Digger". Then he opened the card from Scotland. This one had a picture of a Scots terrier puppy wearing a bright tartan bow. Inside was a message from his cousin Angus and Aunt Bertha.

Albert put both the cards on the mantelpiece, standing one on each side of the marble clock.

The next thing he did was to set the round table with a checked cloth and get his tea ready. He opened the tin of sardines and made a pot of tea. With big chunks of bread and butter and a pot of honey inside him, he was soon feeling quite fresh again, so, after he had cleared away and washed up, he set the little tree in the middle of his table and began to decorate it. He tied the coloured balls on to the branches and twisted the silver tinsel all round the trunk. There was a piece of tinsel to spare so he draped it over the picture of a sailing ship that hung on the wall above the fireplace. Last of all he took out the shining gold star and tied it firmly to the tip of the tree. He pulled the table nearer to the window so that when he put the light on and left the curtains open, the people passing by in the street above could look in and see the little tree shining prettily out at them.

When it was all finished, Albert sat down in his basket chair and poked up the fire. He put on a log of wood from the sackful he had brought home from Mr Higgins' junk-yard and sat back with his toes stretched out to the blaze. He was very happy. Sleepy and a bit stiff, but very happy. The tree shone on the table. The cards looked friendly and cheerful on the mantelpiece.

"I think this is going to be an extra special Christmas," said Albert to himself. He tipped his checked cap over his eyes, leaned back, and began to snore gently.

II

ALBERT GOES MISTLETOEING

Every morning Albert was up early and off on his rounds. He soon learned to handle the letters quickly and he began to watch for unusual stamps and to notice what countries they came from. Best of all he liked it when there was a parcel to deliver, then he would knock on the door until someone came to collect it. If the parcel was gaily wrapped up with bright labels, it made him feel a bit like Father Christmas, especially if he was handing it to a little boy or girl.

On the third morning, Albert was just coming out of the post office with his loaded bag when he heard the clip-clop of a horse's hooves and the rattle of cart-wheels. It was his friend Henry, pulling Mr Higgins' junk cart along the street.

The cart pulled up alongside Albert, and Henry said, "Well, look at you!"

Albert grinned. "I was coming round to show you my armband later on today but I'm glad I met you, because now you have seen me with my bag as well. It's rather fun this, but hard work."

"Tell you what, Albert," said Mr Higgins, "on Sunday you can give your feet a rest and come out with us."

"Thank you very much, Mr Higgins, but I *was* planning to have a lie-in on Sunday."

"We," said Henry, firmly, "all three of us, are going

out into the country to an apple orchard to get a load of mistletoe."

"Mistletoe," said Albert, "from an apple orchard?"

"Mistletoe grows in apple orchards," Henry told him, hoping Albert wouldn't ask him to explain.

Albert would have done, but Mr Higgins interrupted to say that they would pick Albert up very early on Sunday morning and he would be able to see for himself.

When Sunday morning came, Albert had just finished

his breakfast and cleared away when he heard Henry's hooves coming up the road. Without stopping to look round the room, which he knew he really ought to stay and clean up, Albert closed the front door behind him and climbed on to the cart beside Mr Higgins.

It was a bright, cold, frosty morning and Henry's breath hung in misty clouds round his head. "You look like a kettle coming to the boil," Albert told him.

"And you look like a tea cosy in that big muffler of yours," his friend replied.

There wasn't much traffic and they were able to get along quite quickly so it was not very long before they turned into the yard of the farm where they were going to collect the mistletoe.

The farmer was a friend of Mr Higgins called Bert, and Albert politely raised his cap when they were introduced.

The mistletoe had been cut and was lying in a heap in the corner of the yard waiting for them. Albert helped pile it on to the cart but he was secretly a little disappointed that he hadn't seen where it grew. However, Mr Higgins knew that Albert was always interested in everything and he asked Bert if Albert could see the apple orchard and pick a piece for himself.

"Of course you can," said Bert, "come along," and he led the way round the back of the house. Quite close to the house on the other side of a hedge grew a number of old apple trees with thick rough branches that twisted and turned in all directions.

18

"These trees have never been properly pruned and looked after for growing fruit," Bert told him, "and the mistletoe grows on the branches. Look here at this bit," and he showed Albert how the plant was actually growing from a crack in the rough bark of the tree.

"It always grows on trees, sometimes on old oak trees and sometimes apple."

Bert gave Albert a small sharp knife and let him cut a nice bunch which he told him he could keep for himself.

"Thank you very much," said Albert. He looked at the soft green rounded leaves and the little clusters of pearly berries and asked, "Why do people want mistletoe at Christmas? I know they kiss under it at parties and that sort of thing, but why?"

"I don't think anyone is really sure about that. We do know that many hundreds of years ago it was thought to have strange powers and the trees where it grew were sacred and no one was allowed to cut them or even to go near them except the priests. Anyway," he went on with a chuckle, "as you say, it gives people a bit of fun at parties."

They went back to where they had left the others and Bert said they must come in for a "spot of Sunday lunch".

Mr Higgins and Albert could smell the spot of Sunday lunch and were very hungry after their long ride so they agreed happily. They went into the big kitchen, after giving Henry a handful of sweet-smelling hay, which cheered him up quite a bit.

Lunch was roast beef with three kinds of vegetables and Yorkshire pudding. This was followed by apple crumble and a big pot of tea.

It would have been nice to have stayed in front of the crackling fire which was burning wood from one of the old apple trees blown down in a gale, and giving off a lovely warmth and a pleasant smell. But they had a long way to go, so Mr Higgins paid for the load of mistletoe, and with many thanks for the meal and good wishes all round for Christmas, they set off for home.

It was getting a lot colder by now and Mr Higgins said he thought it was quite possible they would have snow for Christmas.

"That would be nice," said Albert, "I like snow, but,"

he went on, "now I come to think of it, I would rather it didn't snow until Christmas Day or I shall have to do my round in it. I've often felt sorry for the poor postmen and milkmen out in all weather and now I know what it is like."

"Yes," Henry called over his shoulder, "we know what it's like too."

"I suppose you do," replied Albert, pulling his warm scarf up a bit nearer to his nose. "Still you have a nice warm stable and Mr Higgins always looks after you."

By the time they reached the London streets they were feeling rather stiff and weary so Albert began to sing carols to cheer them up, though Henry said the only effect they had on *him* was to make him hurry even more to get home. Mr Higgins said that was a good thing and joined Albert in "Good King Wenceslas". After that they worked their way through as much as they could remember of "The Twelve Days of Christmas." Albert was chuckling happily over the way they got all mixed up, when Henry pulled up outside 14 Spoonbasher's Row and he was home.

Albert climbed down off the cart and thanked Mr Higgins very much for the lovely day he'd had. Then he carried his bunch of mistletoe round to the front of the cart and held it as high as he could reach over his friend's head and kissed Henry's soft nose.

"Happy Christmas, Henry," he said.

"Oh, poof," said Henry.

III

ALBERT FOR CHRISTMAS

With the extra money Albert was earning in his job as a postman, he was feeling quite rich, so one afternoon in Christmas week he took his shopping bag and went out

to buy his presents for Henry and Mr Higgins and for his landlady who lived in the flat above.

For some time Albert had been keeping his eyes open for a good horse brass. There was room for one more on the broad band that Henry sometimes wore which hung down from his collar over his strong chest.

Albert was rather interested in horse brasses. He knew that they had been made for many years and that they were probably lucky charms, meant to protect the horses from evil and sickness.

There was one little shop Albert had found and he was heading there now. It was a shop which sold nothing but brass and was so crowded there was hardly room to move between the great trays and jugs from India and little figures from all over the world. The shopkeeper already knew Albert by sight and greeted him when he went into the shop.

"I'm going to buy my brass today," Albert told him.

"Well, I'm glad you didn't get it before," the shop-keeper told him, "because only yesterday I found one that I think you will like."

He showed Albert a brightly polished, flat, round brass. It was a shining sun with eight sunbeams from a circle on which there was a cheerful smiling face.

"Oh, yes, I like that one," Albert said. "It will cheer Henry up when he's feeling grumpy."

Henry's present was carefully wrapped up and put in the bottom of the shopping bag and then Albert spotted rather a nice brass ashtray which had a horse's head in the middle of it.

"That would do for Mr Higgins," he said. "It is a little bit like Henry." So the ashtray went into the bag as well and they were both paid for.

Albert now made his way to another shop where he

carefully chose a pretty blue apron for Mrs Cooper, his landlady.

As he was wandering down the street looking in all the shop windows, Albert suddenly had an idea. He would take a bus down to the West End of London and go to one of the big stores. To the toy department. He would

go and watch people doing their shopping and buying toys to give to children for Christmas.

Albert loved riding on buses through the city and in quite a short time he was looking out of the bus at the big shops with their beautifully decorated windows. One window had rows of sparkling silver trees, another a flight of pure white swans sailing through the air. In one big window he saw a snow scene with models of children in bright clothes playing with a snowman and skating on a frozen pond.

Albert got off the bus and walked along the pavement. He stopped by a small window in which there was a tree decorated with all the things from the carol he and Mr Higgins had been singing: "The Twelve Days of Christmas".

Overhead, as it began to grow darker, thousands of coloured lights suddenly came on. Across the street hung glistening pictures made of lights. They showed scenes from fairy tales, lovely patterns, like frost on a window pane, and they were repeated again and again all the way down the street.

Albert stood and gazed for several minutes and then he turned into one of the big shops and went up in the lift to the toy department.

He wandered slowly around looking at all the lovely toys. Dolls and rabbits and gollywogs. Balls and games and building bricks.

Children were everywhere and their voices were full of excitement as they chose the things they wanted most.

Suddenly a little boy near to Albert pointed to him and said, "*Please*, Mummy, could I have *that* for Christmas? It's the most beautiful Teddy Bear I have ever seen."

Albert turned round. "I beg your pardon," he said.

The little boy's mouth fell open and he turned bright pink. "Oh, excuse me," he said, "I thought— I mean—"

Albert raised his cap politely and said, "My name's Albert and I'm afraid I'm not for sale."

The little boy gazed at him for a moment and then he suddenly smiled and said, "How do you do. I am Ian Curtis and this is my mother."

Albert shook Ian's hand and said that he was very pleased to meet him. "I hope you're not too disappointed," he added.

Ian put out a hand to stroke Albert's honey-coloured fur. "No," he told Albert, "I'm not disappointed."

Mrs Curtis asked Albert if he would like to come and have some tea in the restaurant with them. They went up a flight of stairs and sat at a table in a big room where a man was playing the piano, and had toasted buns, cream cakes and strawberry ice-cream.

Albert enjoyed it very much and he had a lot of fun with Ian who told him he was eight years old.

"We're going to the circus tomorrow night," Ian told Albert, "I wish you could come with us."

"It's very kind of you," said Albert, "but I am going to spend tomorrow evening with my friend Henry. You'll enjoy the circus, I went to one last summer and it was great fun."

"Were there clowns and horses and men on the flying trapeze? What did you like best?" asked Ian.

"The tigers," Albert told him, eagerly. "There were six great big, stripey tigers. They looked so sleek and beautiful and I wanted to take one home with me!"

"Are *we* going to see tigers?" Ian asked his mother.

"Yes, and lions too, I believe."

"Oh, SUPER!"

"I went to a zoo in Ramsgate, when I was down in Kent with Henry," Albert told them, "and I fed a baby lion with a bottle of milk."

Ian gazed at Albert. "You do exciting things, don't you."

"Yes," agreed Albert, "I am very lucky, really."

"Now, young Ian," said his mother, "it's time we were getting you home to bed if you are going to be up late tomorrow." She stood up and began to collect her parcels, then she stopped and thought for a moment.

"There is one way that you could have Albert for Christmas, Ian," she said. She turned to Albert and asked, "Would you like to come and spend Christmas Day with us?"

Albert said, "Yes, thank you. I would like that very much indeed."

A great, big smile spread over Ian's face. "Oh, ALBERT!" he breathed.

"If you tell me where you live, we'll come and fetch you in the car," said Mrs Curtis and Albert explained how to find 14 Spoonbasher's Row.

Albert wished his new friends goodbye down at the main door of the shop because he wanted to go back up to the toy department to buy a present for Ian.

Mrs Curtis looked up at the sky and shivered a little.

"It's getting much colder," she said, "I wouldn't be at all surprised if we have a white Christmas."

"Do you mean snow," asked Ian, excited. "Oh, I do hope it does snow. Don't you, Albert?"

And Albert agreed that snow was about the only thing he needed right then to make his life complete.

IV

ALBERT THE CLOWN

The next day was Christmas Eve and Albert's last day as a postman. He had quite a pile of letters and small parcels to deliver.

When he got back to the post office the man in charge said they were delighted with the way he had worked and that he was an excellent postman. He said he hoped Albert would come again next Christmas.

Albert handed in his bag and a little reluctantly took off his smart armband.

As he was leaving one of the regular postmen called to him. "We wondered if you would do us a favour."

"I will if I can," replied Albert, a little puzzled.

"Well, just after Christmas we have a party for our children. We decorate one of the big rooms upstairs and have a record player and a conjurer and games."

"That sounds fun," said Albert.

"Yes, we usually have a pretty good time and we wondered if you would like to come and if you did would you be Father Christmas and give toys to all the children?"

Albert's mouth fell open. Then he chuckled and said, "Yes, I will. You mean I'm to dress up in a red cloak and beard and all that, don't you?"

"Of course," the postman told him. "We've got all the clothes. There's a hood trimmed with real fur and a long white beard and there will be a sack of toys with one for each child."

"I'm looking forward to it already," said Albert.

"You must come at the beginning of the party and have tea with us. Could you be there by three o'clock on the Saturday after Christmas?"

"Yes, I will and thank you very much for asking me," said Albert and he went off home thinking that what Ian had said was true, he really did do a lot of exciting things and he was a very lucky bear indeed.

It had been arranged that Albert would spend Christmas Eve with Mr Higgins and Henry. Mr Higgins was having Christmas dinner with friends and he was buying

31

the turkey. Albert was going along to help choose it.

He had just finished his fourth slice of bread and honey and was carefully licking the last sticky, delicious drop of honey off his paw, when he heard the cart pull up outside and Mr Higgins calling to him to hurry up.

Quickly Albert rinsed his face and paws under the tap, trotted up the steps to the street and climbed up beside Mr Higgins.

"Do you want to drive?" asked Mr Higgins.

"Yes, please," said Albert, happily. Albert was very good at handling the reins and he knew all about looking after Henry and his harness.

Henry looked round and grinned at his friend. "It'll be nice to be driven by someone who doesn't pull my head off at corners," he remarked.

"That's enough from you," said Mr Higgins, cheerfully. "Any more of your nonsense and we will leave you behind and take the bus."

"Then you'd have to carry your own turkey," Henry told him.

The streets were packed with people doing their last minute Christmas shopping. The cart threaded its way through the traffic, down the twisting narrow streets of London, past the brightly lit shops and the street barrows piled high with holly and mistletoe, nuts and oranges, until they came at last to the big covered market where the poultry was sold.

Hanging in rows were great, fat turkeys, geese with frills of white feathers round their throats and plump chickens. Working hard amongst the birds were the market men in their round straw hats. They were selling the poultry to people for their Christmas dinners and because it was now late on Christmas Eve they were bringing down the prices so as to get rid of all their stock. Lovely big turkeys were being sold off for much less

than they had cost earlier in the day and Mr Higgins hurried to choose one for himself which he managed to buy for even less than the first price the man had asked! He carried the bird back to the cart looking very pleased with himself.

"That will make a lovely dinner," said Albert looking at the fat turkey lying at the back of the cart.

"Would you like to stay and watch the market with

Henry for a little while so that I can have a pint of beer?" asked Mr Higgins.

"Yes, of course," said Albert.

"It will be nice to get away from old Henry's moaning for a few minutes," added Mr Higgins, and he dis-

appeared down the street before Henry could answer. However, he came back a few minutes later with a bottle of orange squash for Albert and three packets of potato crisps for the two friends to share.

Albert stood happily crunching crisps and feeding

every other one to Henry as he watched the busy market.

"It's exciting, isn't it, Henry?"

"Huh?"

"All this."

Henry surveyed the busy scene while he chewed his crisps.

"Suppose so," he grunted.

"Oh, Henry," chuckled Albert, "I sometimes wonder why I like you so much."

Henry reached down and blew in Albert's ear. "I expect it's because I'm always so cheerful," he replied.

Mr Higgins came back and suggested that they drive along to Trafalgar Square and have a look at the big tree.

"That's a good idea," agreed Albert, "I haven't seen it yet." He shook the reins and called, "Come on, Henry. Let's get this waggon rolling. The sheriff and his men are right behind us!"

"Right!" And Henry set off down the street at a brisk trot which took Albert and Mr Higgins completely by surprise and nearly tipped them both over backwards! People jumped out of the way as the cart careered round the corner with its passengers hanging on for their lives!

"All right, Henry," shouted Mr Higgins, "that's enough!"

Henry slowed down at once to his usual steady pace and chortled happily to himself. "That gave you something to think about," he remarked.

Trafalgar Square was full of people singing carols round the huge Christmas tree which had come all the way from Norway. It was completely covered in lights. They found a place at one side of the square and listened

as the crowd sang "Holy Night" and then, slowly and happily, they set off home again.

When they reached the yard, Albert stayed to look after Henry. He unharnessed him and gave him a rub down and then he put out food and water for his friend. While he was doing this, he told Henry all about Ian and how he was going to spend Christmas Day with the

Curtis family. "But I will come round and see you first," he assured Henry.

"I hope you have a wonderful time, Albert," Henry told his friend, nuzzling his ear.

"What will you do while Mr Higgins is out to dinner?"

"Have a good sleep," said Henry, firmly.

V

ALBERT'S CHRISTMAS DAY

When Albert woke up next morning, he yawned sleepily and reached down to the floor for his cap. Then he propped himself up on his pillow and said, "Merry Christmas, Albert, old lad!"

Albert climbed out of bed and padded over to the window. The steps outside, the street and the roofs of the houses opposite were all pure, sparkling white, in the soft gold winter sunshine.

It HAD snowed!

Full of excitement, Albert hurried to eat his breakfast.

Then he gave himself a good wash and combed his fur carefully. On his way to the door he changed his black and white checked everyday cap for his Sunday one with the black, white and blue checks.

Beside the Christmas tree was a pile of parcels all neatly wrapped up in blue paper with golden reindeer all over it and tied with gold string. Albert put three of these parcels into his shopping bag and went out of his

door and up the two flights of steps to the main door of Number Fourteen, where his landlady, Mrs Cooper, lived, and rang the bell.

"Merry Christmas, Mrs Cooper!" he said, handing her one of the parcels.

Mrs Cooper wished Albert a very good Christmas as well and undid the string. "It's lovely, Albert," she smiled when she saw the apron. "Now just wait a minute, because I have something for *you*," and she went away and came back with a parcel wrapped in scarlet paper. Inside was a lovely hand-knitted tea cosy. It had been made from a lot of different colours of wool and was very gay.

"That's very kind indeed of you," Albert told her, "and it is exactly what I need. Thank you so much."

Albert put his present into his bag and went on his way to the junk-yard to see Henry and Mr Higgins. The snow was a few inches thick and he had a wonderful time scuffing his feet through it and sending up little feathery white puffs of snow.

Round at the junk-yard, the piles of old furniture and scrap metal were all covered in snow and looked like weird fairy castles.

Mr Higgins was in the stable giving Henry a rub down.

"Good morning," called Albert, "and a very Happy Christmas to you both."

"The same to you, Albert," they both said and Albert took out Henry's parcel. He undid it for him and showed his friend the horse brass.

Henry was delighted.

"I'll fix it for you later today," Mr Higgins said.

"This is for you," said Albert, passing Mr Higgins the last parcel and Mr Higgins was as pleased as could be with his ashtray.

"It does look a bit like Henry," he agreed, "though I'm not certain that's a *good* thing," he added in a loud whisper so that Henry could hear quite well.

Albert grinned. "Oh, I don't know," he chuckled, "Henry's not such a bad looking chap—er—on his *better* days, that is."

Henry ignored both of them with great dignity.

"This is from Henry and me," said Mr Higgins and handed Albert something wrapped in white tissue paper. It was a long, thick scarf, exactly the same shade of blue as the checks in his Sunday cap.

Albert wrapped the soft warm wool round his neck and up to his ears.

"Thank you very much, indeed," he said simply, and his friends could see that they had chosen just the right thing.

"I must go now," said Albert, "because Mr Curtis and Ian are coming to fetch me."

"Have a wonderful day," they wished him, as he trotted away, with the ends of his new scarf bobbing behind him.

He had only been home long enough to put his new cosy into the cupboard and pick the last parcel off the table, when his new friends arrived, and he went out to meet Mr Curtis.

The Curtis family lived outside the city of London, near Epping forest. They had a big house with a lovely garden.

"It's a good thing it didn't snow too much," said Mr Curtis, as they drove along the white roads, "or it would have been very difficult to come and fetch you."

Mrs Curtis wasn't with Ian and his father; she was busy with the Christmas dinner, but she came to the door to meet them as the car turned in at the gate.

They all went into the big sitting-room where there was a blazing log fire. The room was hung with decorations and in the corner stood a beautiful tree covered with sparkling glass balls and tiny twinkling lights.

Mr Curtis sat Albert down by the fire to get warm and gave him a little glass of ginger wine. Albert found it a bit hot on his tongue, but it went trickling down with a very warm feeling.

"We'll open our presents after dinner," said Mrs Curtis, "because it's all ready and I'm sure everyone is hungry."

They went through to the dining room and sat down. Mrs Curtis carried in a dish on which there was a big, steaming, brown turkey. She put it down in front of Mr Curtis and went back for the vegetables.

It all smelt delicious and Albert found his mouth was watering. He just didn't know where to begin when his plate was put in front of him. But once he got started, there wasn't a word out of him, he just ate and ate and ate, until every scrap of the delicious food had disappeared and then he suddenly looked up at the others and said, "Oh, dear, I'm awfully sorry. It wasn't very polite to wolf it down like that!"

"Nonsense, Albert," laughed Ian's mother. "It's a great pleasure to see my cooking enjoyed so much. Look, Ian and his father have eaten just as much as you have! Now, pass your plate for some more turkey."

Albert and Ian jumped up to help clear away the dishes but then Mrs Curtis made them go back to their places before she brought in the pudding. To Albert's surprise, she first drew the curtains so that the only light came from the candles on the table and then she carried in a dish on which stood a dark Christmas pudding covered in blue flame!

She put it down on the table and blew out the flame, then she looked up and saw the expression on Albert's face and laughed.

"Did you think it was on fire? We pour brandy over the pudding and set light to it. It makes the pudding taste even better." She passed a big helping to Albert and told him to help himself to the brandy butter. This was a sugary, crunchy, hard sauce that melted over the hot pudding and was absolutely gorgeous.

Albert had two helpings of pudding and wondered blissfully if he was ever going to be able to move again!

Afterwards, with nuts and tangerines in dishes on a low table in case anyone had an inch of room to spare, they sat in front of the fire and listened to a carol service from a chapel in Cambridge.

When they had recovered slightly, Mr Curtis took the parcels from the foot of the tree and handed them around. Ian was thrilled with his presents. He had a football and some books and Albert had brought him a toy train which he thought was "super".

"If you like to go and look in the cupboard under the stairs, you will find your special present," his father told him.

"Come with me, Albert," yelped Ian and dragged Albert out of his chair into the hall, where they opened the door of the cupboard and found a brand new, beautiful sledge!

"Oh, Gosh!" he breathed, "isn't that just—oh, GOSH!" He raced back to his father and mother and hugged them. "Can we go out with it now?" he begged.

"In a few minutes, when we've given Albert *his* presents," said his mother and Ian said, "Sorry, Albert.

Look, these are for you." Albert opened his two parcels
and in one of them was a lovely rich fruit cake which
smelt heavenly and in the other was a great big jar of
thick, golden honey. "These are LOVELY," he told them.
"It's very good of you."

"We just wanted to say how pleased we are to have
met you," Mrs Curtis told him and Albert felt quite hot
round the tips of his ears.

Ian rushed to put on his coat and cap now and brought
Albert his scarf. "Come on, Albert, let's go and try the
sledge."

Behind the house there was a sloping piece of ground which was perfect for sledging and there was quite a lot of snow.

They pulled the bright sledge up to the top of the slope and climbed on. Off they went! Skimming over the snow with the cold wind streaming past their ears. Ian wasn't too good at steering the sledge and when they

reached the bottom, they went sideways and tumbled off into the snow! They rolled over spluttering and laughing and brushed the snow off themselves before setting off up the slope to try again.

They had a wonderful time, but it began to get dark and cold very quickly and suddenly there was a fierce wind blowing and a flurry of thick snow in their faces.

"Come along in, you two," called Mr Curtis from the garden.

"Oh, must we," begged Ian, but then he shivered and said, "Still, it is cold and horrid now, isn't it, Albert," and Albert agreed that the sky looked dark and nasty.

"It's going to snow again, hard," Mr Curtis told them, as they went inside. "Your mother and I think it would be a good idea if Albert could stay the night."

"That would be marvellous. Could you, Albert?" asked Ian.

"If you are sure it's not too much trouble, I would like to very much," said Albert and they all went into the sitting-room to drink tea and eat Christmas cake in front of the log fire.

"This is so nice," said Albert, toasting his toes, "it's so CHRISTMASSY!"

VI

ALBERT AND THE KNAVE OF HEARTS

By the time they went to bed it was bitterly cold and
the wind was howling round the house, sending flurries
of snow against the windows, but Albert slept soundly,
on the couch in the sitting-room, covered by two warm
blankets, and when he woke in the morning it had
stopped snowing and the garden was a silver fairyland.

While Albert was having breakfast with Ian and his
father and mother, they heard a loud rumbling noise
outside and from the window they could see a snow
plough trundling up the road, pushing the snow to the
sides and clearing a path for traffic.

"Thank goodness for that," remarked Mr Curtis, "I
wondered how we would be able to get out. It's a good
thing we live on the main road; if we can't get the car

out, at least we are not too far from the station. After breakfast I'll shovel the snow off the front path and perhaps you two would like to give me a hand."

"Yes, of course, we will, Daddy," said Ian, "and then we can get the sledge out again, can't we, Albert?"

"Well, I would like that very much," said Albert, "but I must think about getting home."

"Are you in a hurry to get home for anything special?" asked Mrs Curtis and Albert told her he wasn't, but that

they had been very kind and he didn't want to be any trouble.

"You're no trouble at all and Ian loves having you here." Then Mrs Curtis went on, "You see, if we can get through the snow we are going this afternoon to the pantomime in town and as we have the stage box which seats four, you might like to come with us and then you could go straight home from there."

"Yes, please," said Albert, excitedly, "I went to a panto last year and had a lot of fun. It was 'Mother Goose'."

"This one is 'The Queen of Hearts' and I think it will be very good. Well, that's settled, then," she said. "Now go and help Daddy sweep away the snow, and then you can spend the rest of the morning playing in it."

With caps over their ears and warm scarves pulled tight, Albert and Ian followed Mr Curtis out to the garage, plodding through the thick snow. They collected a shovel and two spades and set to work on the path and the front steps.

It was good fun and they were soon so warm they actually took off their scarves. Mrs Curtis brought out mugs of hot chocolate and between them they soon had the way clear from the house to the road.

Ian went to get the sledge and they set off up to the top of the slope and this time Mr Curtis went with them and showed them how to steer the sledge properly, but it didn't always work and they all had a good laugh when Mr Curtis himself came off the sledge halfway down and rolled over and over in the snow!

"Why don't we make a snowman?" he suggested when he had got his breath back. So they went back to the garden and made a big heap of snow ready to model into a snowman.

"What shall we make?" asked Ian, "I know! How about a teddy bear! With a cap on."

"Now, now, Ian, I'm not sure that is very polite," said his father. "Albert might think you were making fun of him."

"Oh, no, that's all right," said Albert, "I don't mind."

"Besides, teddy bears are such nice things," Ian explained, "it would be a bit like making a statue of him!"

"Right then," laughed Mr Curtis, "let's put up a statue of Albert," and they did. They built a big teddy bear and Mrs Curtis found them an old cap and scarf to put on it. By the time lunch was ready, there was a snow-Albert standing in the garden with pebbles for eyes and big white ears.

They went laughing into the dining room and sat down, very hungry, to a good meal of cold turkey and fried potatoes, followed by mince-pies.

Mr Curtis listened to the weather forecast and learned that no more snow was expected that day, so he decided that it would be safe to go into town on the train to the pantomime.

At the theatre Albert was very interested when they went into the stage box. It had its own special door and there were four chairs which they could arrange any way they liked. It was close up to the stage.

Mr Curtis had a parcel with him and he gave it to his wife. Inside was an enormous box of chocolates which she passed round to them all. "I think it will just about last the afternoon," she said, watching Ian carefully choosing his favourite.

They watched the orchestra coming up through a little door, followed by the conductor who led them in a nice, noisy, cheerful piece of music. As soon as it was finished they started straight off with another piece and the curtain went up on the scene of a village square filled with girls and boys dancing and singing.

Steadily eating chocolates, Albert and Ian settled down to watch the pantomime. They roared with laughter at all the comedian's jokes. They shouted out to warn the princess that the demon king was just behind her and they joined in all the songs they were invited to join in.

Albert specially liked the pantomime horse and, although he knew it was really two men, he told Ian it was rather like his friend Henry and he decided to see if Henry could dance like that.

In the interval they had ice cream, and Mrs Curtis wondered out loud where they put it all! She said Ian never seemed to stop eating but she reassured Albert that all teddy bears should be plump, and would he like another chocolate?

Towards the end of the second half there was a scene

where the Knave of Hearts and two of his friends were in the kitchen baking tarts. It was very funny because they did everything wrong and fell into the big mixing bowl and covered themselves with flour. The knave got jam all over his face and Albert roared with laughter.

When they had made the pretend pastry, they began to throw it at each other. It was made of pieces of white plastic foam but it looked just like real pastry. Albert was laughing so much they could hear him on the stage. The knave looked up to the box and saw Albert. The next thing Albert knew, a lump of the pastry dropped into his lap!

Quickly he grabbed it and threw it back at the knave and in a moment the battle on the stage had spread to the stage box as the three men tossed plastic pastry backwards and forwards to Ian and Albert. Even Mr and Mrs Curtis joined in and the audience thought it was very funny and rocked with laughter.

When the curtain went down on that scene there was quite a mess to clear up on the stage and the stage-hands must have worked very fast because when the curtain went up again a few minutes later for the last act, the scene was the inside of the king's palace with a wide staircase, golden pillars round the sides and all the chorus lined up in lovely glittering costumes.

One by one the principal characters in the pantomime came down the stairs and were clapped by the audience as they took up their places on either side. When the knave came down in a brand new costume, just like

the figure on the playing cards, he got an extra special clap. He waved to Albert and Ian and made them stand up to take a bow as well!

When it was all over, Mr Curtis managed to get hold of a taxi and he said they would drop Albert off at his home and then go on to the station.

"Won't you come in and have some tea with me before you go home," asked Albert, "I've got this lovely cake and the honey and everything else we need is in the cupboard."

So they drove through the snowy streets of London, right down to the East End and stopped outside 14 Spoonbasher's Row.

"Somebody's cleared the snow off my steps!" exclaimed Albert. "I expect that was Mr Cooper, he's very kind."

On the doorstep there was a bottle of milk and a sack of firewood from Mr Higgins.

They went inside and Ian and his mother looked round the room while Albert put the kettle on and Mr Curtis put a match to the fire.

"It's a lovely cosy room," said Mrs Curtis.

Albert sat on the bed with Ian so that Ian's parents could have the two chairs.

"I don't usually have more than one visitor," he explained, "but it's nice to have a real party."

They had bread and honey, slices of fruit cake and big cups of tea, and warmed themselves at the crackling fire that burned up quickly with some of the wood Henry had brought.

"Mr Higgins often brings me wood from his yard, because he chops up furniture that he can't sell and I do little jobs for him to pay for it."

"I have a feeling that you often do little jobs for people even if you don't get paid for it," remarked Mrs Curtis, gently, and Albert felt his ears tingling as they always did when anyone said something nice to him.

It had been arranged that the taxi would come back for the Curtis family in an hour and there it was, tooting its horn outside.

Albert jumped up to shake hands with his new friends and say, "I've enjoyed myself so much, I don't know how to thank you."

Mr Curtis looked at his little son Ian and at Ian's mother.

"You have nothing to thank us for, Albert," he said, "I know we have all loved having you and I can't remember when I laughed as much as I have these past two days!"

VII

ALBERT AT THE PARTY

Albert went shopping the next morning and the weather was terrible. An icy wind had left the North Pole that morning and headed straight for Spoonbasher's Row, without stopping on the way.

Albert battled with the door of the butcher's shop and struggled to close it again.

"Whew!" he gasped, "Isn't this awful!"

"Haven't seen anything like it for years," agreed the butcher. "I know what *I* would do, if I were a bear."

"What's that?" asked Albert.

"Hibernate."

"I beg your pardon?"

"Hibernate. You know, go to sleep for the winter."

"Oh, yes," said Albert. "It's a different sort of bears that do that, but it's not a bad idea, as you say."

Rather thoughtfully, Albert finished his shopping and bought a little more than usual of things like his favourite sausages and bread and butter. He even bought himself a small bottle of the ginger wine which he had found to be very warming.

He fought his way home against the wind, slipping and slithering over the frozen hard, churned-up snow. He struggled to close the front door behind him and drew the curtain across it.

As Albert put away his food and filled the kettle, he thought about the bears who went to sleep all through the cold weather and he said to himself, "Why not?" He poured out a cup of tea and told himself he had nothing important to do until the party on Saturday and that this was one of the nicest, laziest ideas he had ever had!

He built up a roaring fire from the wood Mr Higgins had brought him and made a lovely pile of hot buttered toast. After he had finished his tea—he went to bed!

And there he stayed.

For the next three days, while the cold winds whistled round the streets and the snow became more and more lumpy and frozen and dirty, the way it does in towns, all that could be seen of Albert, except when he was getting his breakfast or supper and making up the fire, was the tip of his nose, peeping out from a pile of bedclothes. He slept and snoozed and ate and dozed.

When Saturday morning came round, Albert woke up properly and decided that he had had enough of this hibernation business, but he did feel marvellous and fit for anything, and what was more—"The sun's shining!" he said in surprise.

And so it was. The sky was blue, most of the snow had been cleared away off the streets and Albert couldn't wait to get out into the fresh air, and go and see Henry.

Full of beans, he cleaned up his room and gave himself a really good wash, and before very long he was turning into the yard where Henry was standing with his head in his feed-bag.

"Hello, Henry," said Albert, "how are you?"

"I'm fine, thank you," said Henry, "and you seem very chirpy this morning. What have you been doing during this cold weather?"

"Sleeping," explained Albert, cheerfully.

"Sleeping!" Henry snorted. "Some people have all the luck. Wish *I* could sleep like that, but I have to work for my living."

"Poor old Henry," laughed Albert. Anyway, horses don't hibernate—at least I don't *think* they do."

"Don't WHAT? Whatever it is, you can bet horses have to do it."

"Hibernating is sleeping all through the cold weather, like squirrels and frogs and—er—"

"Teddy Bears?" enquired Henry.

"Um—well—anyway, it was fun and now I'm going to a party."

He told Henry all about the party that afternoon and Henry had a good chuckle at the thought of Albert dressed up in the Father Christmas costume.

When Mr Higgins came out into the yard a little later, Albert was teaching Henry how to dance like a panto-mime horse and he was in time to see Albert, helpless with laughter, propping Henry up while the horse tried to cross his front and back legs at the same time.

At tea-time that afternoon, Albert, wearing the gay tartan cap he had bought in Scotland, was sitting down at a long table, surrounded by happy children, tucking into jellies, ice-cream, sugary buns and cake. There were crackers with paper hats in them to pull and funny jokes to read out.

After they had finished tea the mothers of the children and their fathers, who were all postmen, cleared away the tea things and sat everybody down in rows of chairs to watch the conjurer.

This was a man wearing evening dress and a long cloak lined with splendid red satin. He wore a top hat and the first thing he did was to show them all that the hat was empty and then take six white doves out of it that flew around the room! When the birds had been called back and put into a cage, he put a cloth over the cage and made them all disappear.

Albert and the children and the fathers and mothers all sat fascinated as he turned silk scarves into rabbits, made balls appear and disappear in mid air, or come out of the children's ears, and did all sorts of wonderful tricks. He ended up by pulling yards and yards of coloured silk out of an empty glass tumbler.

When the conjurer had gone, the chairs were moved

back and some of the fathers started the children playing games.

One of the men came up and spoke to Albert quietly. It was time for him to creep away and change.

He was taken to another room and dressed up in a long red robe with white fur trimmings, black boots and a red hood with fur round his face. A long white beard was hooked over his ears like spectacles, but the moustache part had to be cut off because it lay firmly over his nose!

Round his waist he fastened a black belt which he had a bit of trouble with because Albert didn't have much of a waist. The two men who were helping him did their best not to laugh because, in spite of the slipping belt, he did look rather like a kindly Father Christmas.

Carrying a sack full of exciting looking parcels, Albert went back to the bigger room where the lights had been turned down and a record of "Jingle Bells" was playing.

As he came in the door, the children all went, "Oooh!"

Albert put on a very good act and in a gruff voice he spoke to the children and asked them if they had been good, because if they had he was going to give them their presents.

Of course, the children all told him that they had been very good indeed and so he sat down and began to take out the parcels.

There was one for each child and the name was written

on it. Albert called out their names and they came forward to get their gift. They all said, "Thank you, Father Christmas," properly and Albert enjoyed himself very much indeed.

When the sack was empty, the lights were turned up again and another record was put on so that the children could play musical chairs. Albert sat watching them, stroking his beard, and a little girl, who was too busy nursing her new doll to play with the others, came and climbed into his lap.

She sat there happily holding her doll and then she suddenly pulled Albert's head down and gave him a big kiss on the cheek.

"Thank you EVER so much for my dolly and all the lovely things you put into my stocking on Christmas Day," she said. "I've had SUCH a wonderful Christmas."

"So have I," said Father Albert Christmas.